THE
EXTRAORDINARY
LIFE OF A
MEDIOCRE
JOCK

THE EXTRAORDINARY LIFE OF A MEDIOCRE JOCK

TED A. KLUCK

ILLUSTRATED BY
DANIEL HAWKINS

HARVEST HOUSE PUBLISHERS
EUGENE, OREGON

Cover design by Kyler Dougherty

Interior design by Chad Dougherty

Published in association with the literary agency of Wolgemuth & Associates, Inc.

HARVEST KIDS is a registered trademark of The Hawkins Children's LLC. Harvest House Publishers, Inc., is the exclusive licensee of the federally registered trademark HARVEST KIDS.

The Extraordinary Life of a Mediocre Jock

Copyright © 2018 Ted Kluck
Artwork © 2018 by Daniel Hawkins
Published by Harvest House Publishers
Eugene, Oregon 97408
www.harvesthousepublishers.com

ISBN 978-0-7369-7135-5 (hardcover)
ISBN 978-0-7369-7136-2 (eBook)

Library of Congress Cataloging-in-Publication Data

Names: Kluck, Ted, author. | Hawkins, Daniel, illustrator.
Title: The extraordinary life of a mediocre jock / Ted Kluck ; artwork by
   Daniel Hawkins.
Description: Eugene, Oregon : Harvest House Publishers, [2018] | Summary:
   Indiana seventh-grader Flex, average at everything, yearns to be cool, and
   with help from his parents, his football team, a mysterious girl named KK,
   and a little faith, he may escape obscurity.
Identifiers: LCCN 2017035992 (print) | LCCN 2017047289 (ebook) | ISBN
   9780736971362 (ebook) | ISBN 9780736971355 (hardcover)
Subjects: LCSH: Graphic novels. | CYAC: Graphic novels. |
   Popularity—Fiction. | Middle schools—Fiction. | Schools—Fiction. |
   Christian life—Fiction. | BISAC: JUVENILE FICTION / Religious / Christian
   / General. | JUVENILE FICTION / Comics & Graphic Novels / General.
Classification: LCC PZ7.7.K63 (ebook) | LCC PZ7.7.K63 Ext 2018 (print) | DDC
   741.5/31—dc23
LC record available at https://lccn.loc.gov/2017035992

Printed in the United States of America

18 19 20 21 22 23 24 25 26 / BVG-CD / 10 9 8 7 6 5 4 3 2 1

For Tristan, Maxim, and the real "Pops."

I HAVE TO POOP (OR, WHAT ANXIETY FEELS LIKE)

For me it is a rapid flushing of the face.

Meaning that my face gets, like, really, really hot and I feel like I have to poop. I get this anxious feeling several times each day, including (but not limited to) the following three occasions:

1. Right before band practice.

My band teacher is roughly 150 years old, has a face like a basset hound, and hates me. I play saxophone, meaning that for 55 minutes I sit and hold a saxophone and try to look like I know what I'm doing.

The people who sit on either side of me are girls who have really hot names like "Krissy" and "Elaine." Names that aren't hot themselves but are made hotter because the girls are in eighth grade.

They smell like hair spray and lip gloss, and I find that really intoxicating. To date, I have said zero words to Krissy because another thing happens when I get super nervous—my mouth gets dry and I have trouble making words. So, yeah, some challenges there.

My mom put me in the band because in Empty Factory, Indiana (that's my town), the "good kids" take band and get into classes with other good kids and good teachers. Everybody else is a "bad kid." I'm not sure this is true, but it's the prevailing wisdom in Empty Factory.

Aside: I'm Flex. I'm in seventh grade. I don't really know where the nickname "Flex" came from.

Actually, I do. I'm sorry I lied just then.

It came a year ago when I discovered push-ups and started doing hundreds of them (along with sit-ups) in my room each morning and night.

Full disclosure: I struggle with chin-ups because I'm a bigger guy. I can only do three.

Anyway. I started with push-ups, and apparently, according to my friend Doug Smith (nickname: Dougie Fresh), every time I walked by a mirror, a window, a shiny piece of metal, or anything else that could reflect an image, I would flex (like, my biceps or triceps) a little.

Middle school kids can be ruthless when it comes to nicknames. Do I love the nickname? I should probably say no—because saying no would be the humble, self-effacing, and right thing to do—except that I kind of like it.

Empty Factory is in the middle of nowhere, in Indiana. It's about 90 minutes by car north of Indianapolis (where the rich kids shop) and about 30 minutes north of Muncie (where the regular kids shop). We shop at Murphy's, which is a department store in downtown Empty Factory. Sometimes we make it to the Muncie Mall, where I'm mortified if anyone I know sees me with my mom (see: anxiety).

As you can imagine, Empty Factory got its name because of all the empty factories we have in town.

If we had more hipsters in our town, these buildings would be repurposed as coffee shops or "gastropubs," which is just a gross-sounding name for a restaurant. We have three stoplights, a public pool, and lots of tanning parlors. Our chief export is super-tan girls who go to college at Ball State in Muncie.

Everybody wants to get out of Empty Factory. My way out is going to be football. I'm probably going to play in the NFL.

Playing in the NBA is my fallback, with baseball a distant third.

AM I COOL?

Well, I'm 12 years old and writing a memoir, so that right there probably disqualifies me from being cool.

I've always liked reading and writing. What can I say?

In the pantheon of Nerdy Kids Who Write Books, everybody is doing apoca-

lyptic fiction or trying to write their own versions of *The Hobbit*. But I'm not a nerd—in either the cool or uncool sense of the word. Cool nerds listen to bands you've never heard of and obsess about video games. Uncool nerds are like cool nerds except that they skip the bands and just obsess about the video games.

That about sums up the nerd situation.

But what I really love is football (and to a lesser degree, basketball and baseball and track and professional wrestling—which I don't admit to in mixed company). I live for football, which brings me to Anxious Have-to-Poop Scenario number two:

2. Right before football practice.

Our locker room at Empty Factory Middle School is

actually in the boiler room. We put on our shoulder pads underneath asbestos pipes that will probably one day kill us.

In fact, I think I feel a cough coming on (coughs). This doesn't seem to bother anyone except me, and I don't say anything about it out loud.

Two people who are cooler than me are our star running back, Scottie (nickname: Maverick, or Mav) and our quarterback, Fordo.

Scottie has great shoes, wears a gold chain and totally pulls it off, and is dating Krissy from band.

When you're a seventh grader dating an eighth grader, you're automatically cool. You're, like, grandfathered into being cool forever. Our kids will tell our grandkids about you. That's how cool you are.

But football really stresses me out, even though it's the thing I love more than any other thing in the world. I know I should say I love God more than football…and I do. I mean, I do. Except that football is the thing I think about and dream about. When I get home from practice, I lay out my jersey on the floor and put on my headphones and just dream about football. About what I'll do in the jersey.

Regarding the jersey: I was assigned number 82, which is a really uncool number, but I traded with my buddy Carl Hoppe (pronounced "Hoppy") on the bus and got number 88, which is much cooler. 88 is a number you can do something with.

Coach has a perpetually red face, but not because he's nervous. It's because he's Intense. In Coach Wood's world, there are two kinds of people—people who are Intense and have Pride, and people who lack Intensity and Pride. (Spoiler alert: You don't want to be the second kind of person.)

I'm the first kind, or at least I'm trying to be. I'm always fully dressed in my uniform 15 minutes before practice because I have both Intensity and Pride. I study the playbook at home. I usually ask for it really early, like in March.

I'm not the most athletic guy, but I work really, really hard. There are some guys like this in the NFL, and not surprisingly, they are my favorite players. I'm a starter at tight end and outside linebacker.

Why am I this nervous before an average Thursday practice? I have no idea. The cool kids (like Mav and Fordo) aren't like this. They wait until the last minute to get their uniforms on, and Mav is currently showing Fordo something on his iPhone. They're both laughing.

Cool kids get to bring their iPhones to school. My parents won't let me.

BULLYBALL: FLEX HAS AN "ALTERCATION"

oach Wood played on the most successful high
school football team in Empty Factory Bruins football history. They won the 1988 state championship, and everybody on that team immediately
achieved godlike status around town.

Young Coach Wood

Their money is no good in places like the Scotch Mist (a restaurant) and Subway (a Subway). This means they rarely have to pay for their food. Coach talks about that team often (meaning, all the time), and the greatest compliment you can get is if he compares you to a player on that team. When Coach isn't coaching our team, he's teaching driver's education and US history, which usually involves him playing a documentary and sleeping in the back of the classroom.

The whistle blows after warm-ups, and we gather at the middle of the field between two blocking dummies. It's time for the Oklahoma drill, which is also (depending on who you ask) called the Nutcracker drill, or simply Hamburger.

It's a drill that pits two guys against each other, about five yards apart, between the dummies. When the whistle blows, the two guys come out of their stances and smash into each other.

It's not complicated.

My dad, Pops, always tells me to be first in drills because coaches like this. Pops had always been my coach until this season. Pops played college football at a small school in Wisconsin and was all-conference. Afterward, he played semipro football, played for a season in an arena football league, and coached for a long time.

My favorite thing to do with Pops is to go out to an empty field behind our house and run pass patterns every night. My second-favorite thing is eating

cereal and watching *SportsCenter* with Pops every morning.

Everything I know about football I learned from Pops. Everything I learned about Intensity, I learned from Coach Wood, who has a vein in his forehead that looks like it could burst at any moment and start squirting blood everywhere.

This is one of those life moments in which it's important to respond. Being first means a lot in this context. It means you're not soft, which in Coach's economy is right down there with being a communist. If you're soft you might as well turn in your gear and go try out for the cheerleading squad.

I step between the bags.

This is a good time to explain that there's a kid at school who has been picking on me. And that the reason he picks on me is that my ears stick out. I consider myself a decent-looking guy except that my ears have grown faster than the rest of my body. They stick out. It is what it is (which is a thing football players say).

This is Coach-speak for "Why are you so full of Intensity and Pride today?" I smile behind my face mask.

"Call somebody out, Flex!" I stare at him blankly for a moment until I realize that he wants me to pick somebody to go against in the Nutcracker drill. I don't even have to think about it.

Coppock is the guy who has been making fun of my ears. And by "making fun of," I mean flipping. He'll walk up behind me in school and just sort of flip my ears in a way that makes them red and sore for the rest of the day. And because punching him would get me expelled, I don't do anything about it. This is my chance to do something about it.

Full disclosure: He also makes fun of my last name a lot. Admittedly, it is funny.

Coppock is standing with a group of guys and laughing because when you're a bully and are semicool, you're always standing with a group of guys and laughing. It's just what you do.

He ambles out between the bags and stands in front of me. His jersey is big and baggy, and he's breathing fast through his mouthpiece. I can tell he's nervous now. So am I. We both look like kids who are pretending to be grown up.

This is a strange moment that sometimes occurs in football. What I instinctively want, more than anything, is to go home and have dinner with my mom and dad and pretend that none of this is happening. But I also want to beat Coppock in this drill and then beat him into a pulp.

Today, that impulse wins out.

Coach blows his whistle to signal the end of the drill, but I just keep hitting Coppock with my hands and forearms. Finally, I feel a big, meaty hand on the back of my shoulder pads, and Coach is pulling me off.

His eyes are bloodshot and crazed-looking. But (and I may be making this up) I think I see something satisfied in them (the eyes).

"Take a run! Five laps around the field!"

Is he mad at me for showing Intensity and Pride? I'm not sure. But as I take off for my run, he looks at me and winks. He smiles a little. For the first time all day, I feel good. I don't feel anxious at all anymore.

I LIKE YOUR SHOES

After practice I stand on a stoop outside the school, holding my dirty laundry in a mesh bag and trying to figure out what to do with my other hand while I wait for my ride.

What looks cool, in terms of standing around? Thumb hooked in pocket? If I had a Zippo lighter, I could flip it open and closed. I've heard of people doing that. I can't diddle with my iPhone because my parents keep it at home during the day. I'm certain the saxophone case next to me on the ground isn't helping me in this area (looking cool).

Behind me the door opens, and Tiffany emerges, smelling like someplace exotic and looking conventionally beautiful except for one green eye and one blue eye (which to me just makes the whole thing—her—more compelling).

Which brings me to my final anxiety-addled situation:

3. When I see Tiffany in any context.

At the mall.

At the grocery store.

At school.

The complicated thing is that I want to see her but I really don't want to see her. My physical response is a dry mouth, an elevated heart rate, and a red face. This is based on, I guess, a fundamental belief that she is better than me, which isn't founded in any kind of reality because I don't really know her at all. She's taken on a mythic quality in the same way a famous athlete I don't know also has a mythic quality.

I instinctively pick a piece of sidewalk and stare intently at it as she walks by.

On the positive side, I have a post-practice glow about me. A gladiatorial post-practice glow.

Not only did I just practice and shower, I just won a fight and vanquished my arch-nemesis, Coppock. An archnemesis who, granted, I'll have to see again at school  tomorrow. If I was ever going to say anything to Tiffany, it would be now.

But I've got nothing. Nothing. None of the rehearsed lines sound any good anymore. So I just stand and stare at the concrete.

She's alone, which is shocking. Usually girls like this are transported from place to place by a throng of adoring and slightly less hot friends. I'm alone too. I guess that makes us alone together, and the vibe is different because neither of us is performing for anybody else.

My face feels like it's on fire. I raise my eyes to meet hers. One green, one blue. They really are magnificent eyes. I would like to one day receive a note from her—folded all neatly and with x's and o's on it. Smelling faintly of her perfume. If I was more courageous, I'd find a way to text her. But what would I say? I'm not that guy.

In church, the pastor talks a lot about genuinely loving Christ and how that's a good thing. Again, I struggle with this. I know without a doubt that I love football. I love my parents. I love the idea of Tiffany or someone like her. I think that's why it's so hard to actually have love for Christ. I'm not sure how it's supposed to feel. I've asked a few people, and nobody can really tell me. I guess what I'm waiting for is the feeling—where I feel the same way about Christ as I do about football or Tiffany. That's probably a disrespectful way of talking about it, but it's honest.

Just as quickly, I look back down at my shoes. First edition Air Jordans. Red and black with the white base. They were a big sacrifice for my parents. I knew they couldn't afford them, but they went for it anyway. They really are magnificent shoes.

POPS

When I get home, Pops is in the garage, where he often is. It's where our weight set lives and where Pops spends a lot of his evening hours.

Like I said before, Pops played football in college and a little bit after that. Sometimes I'll take his old jerseys out of the closet and lay them on the floor and put on my headphones…and just dream. Now Pops has a real job (he's a flight instructor), but I know he still dreams of football. He can't turn it off. Neither can I.

His body is like a road map of pain. He has a plate and ten screws in his right leg. The scar is straight and pink and about seven inches long. Actually it's exactly seven inches. I measured it one time while he was napping. He has a scar on his collarbone where they had to put in a rod after he broke it in a semipro game.

"I'm damaged goods, kiddo," he says when he sees me eyeing the scars. I know he doesn't mean it though.

Nobody works as hard as Pops. The garage is a shrine to his hard work. He sweats in little droplets on the floor. Overhead presses. Bench presses. Squats. Pops trains like he's still playing for a team even though he hasn't played for more than 15 years. The weights clang when he drops them to the floor.

The boombox pumps Guns N' Roses' *Appetite for Destruction*. Pops isn't one of those dads who tries to be cool around my friends. He's cool without even trying.

He strips weight off. He does reps with 225 but drops it down to about 100 for me. And he keeps his hands on the bar the whole time. It goes without saying, but I love lifting with my dad.

I can tell it's taken a lot of restraint for him to wait this long to ask. My dad's great struggle in life is trying not to be a Little League dad. Our town is full of them. Pops calls them "The Dead Coaches Society," which I'm pretty sure is a reference to an old movie. They stand along a fence in their name-brand sweats, talking about the glory days and how stupid the coach is and how much better the teams would be if they were in charge.

Pops never sits or stands with them. During games he sits alone, looking nervous and slightly miserable. My mom, Mimi, doesn't like sitting with him.

Mimi is a saint who totally doesn't understand the existence of football. She doesn't understand why Pops and I care so much about it.

They never, ever fight...but when they do, it's about football. And just to be clear, by "fight," I mean Pops gets frustrated about a game and Mimi listens up to a certain point but then gets mad at him for being mad. Nobody is throwing plates at anybody's head or anything. It's not that kind of fighting.

Aside: Mimi, I know for a fact, actually *loves* God—like in a true affection sort of way. Everybody *says* they love God. Everybody (pretty much) goes to church. Everybody (myself included) knows the right stuff to say about God. But I can tell Mimi actually loves Him. She reads her Bible every morning and fills huge notebooks with her notes about it. She reads Scripture to me and prays with me when I'm anxious at night and can't sleep (which is often). I know she wants me to love God too, and I think it worries her that I seem like I don't.

Pops seems to love God too, although he's a little less vocal about it than Mimi. I see him reading his Bible every morning before breakfast.

What I don't know is if Pops will be mad at me for getting in a practice fight and having to run laps. He can tell something is wrong.

Pops used to start a fight on the first day of practice every season, just as a matter of principle. I think I'll be okay.

I take special care to be neither excited nor especially emotional about how I say this. The fact of the matter is, I'm kind of excited, kind of freaked out, and kind of nervous about seeing Coppock at school tomorrow.

Pops knows about Coppock and the ear-flipping and the name stuff. He's silent for a minute.

And that, in a nutshell, is Pops.

6

SCHOOL THE NEXT DAY

There's always a little bit of school-related nervousness, even on the best day. But today is different. It's the first day I've gone to school after a practice fight. The fact that you win a practice fight doesn't immediately turn you into Superman. My friend George Blake's sister drives us to school, and even she knows about the fight. Why? I'm not sure. It may be because Empty Factory is a tiny town, and word travels fast.

I slide awkwardly into the backseat with my saxophone case (not cool).

The fact that I even register on the, like, mental radar of George Blake's sister is a huge deal. I feel a little more like Superman. This might be a good day.

Still, my heart pounds a little when Coppock walks down the hall toward me with a kid named Corey who is tall and has braces and is always sneering (but it may be the braces). There's a rumor going around that Corey spent a year in juvie or something.

I'm headed toward English class with Dr. Warren.

Coppock slows down by my locker and offers me a fist-pound, which is the universal sign for "we're cool." Corey sneers some more.

Relief. Massive relief.

Dr. Warren insists that we all take her and her class super seriously. But she wears her hair in a side ponytail, which makes her look like a Disney character.

Dr. Warren is the only teacher at Empty Factory Middle School with her doctorate, and as such, she insists that everyone calls her Dr. Warren. Probably even her husband calls her that.

Also, my friend Zach thinks she looks like an anime. In fact, he draws her as a flying anime character and slides it over onto my desk.

I laugh uncontrollably.

All she has to say is "Flex." My face flushes. Oh man.

See, I'm a kid who has never really been in trouble because I'm what people refer to as a people pleaser. That's why the practice fight was such new territory for me. Getting caught reading a note in class is new territory too.

Dr. Warren, thankfully, knows I'm a people pleaser, and she backs off. She also kind of knows, I think, that I secretly love her class, but because of my position on the football team I'm required to kind of act like I don't love it. This is dumb, and we both know it. This gives us kind of a bond.

Dr. Warren also has this thing where she just sort of stares at you. It's like she missed the social skills thing where staring was sort of discouraged. Sometimes I think the stares are friendly-ish...other times I think she might want to kill me. This is one of those times.

She uses words like "edification."

Another note from Zach, which reads, "Do you think she's hot?" The arrow is pointing at Dr. Warren. I half smile. Zach is killing it today.

WHAT'S A READER'S THEATER?

When you're in middle school, going into the high school building for any reason is a big deal. The floors are shinier. The trophy case is bigger and a little more intimidating. The 1988 3A State Football Championship trophy sits like a shrine, right in the middle of it.

To be honest, I always stop and gawk at it a little. There's a photograph of Coach Wood in his uniform, above the words "Central Indiana Conference—All-Conference Player." There's a slightly deflated football that has been painted over with the final score of the game: Empty Factory 31, Tipton 28.

The hallway smells like popcorn and industrial-strength cleaner (piney). There are high school kids walking around in their letterman jackets, all of whom have no idea who I am.

I see Dr. Warren directing people into the auditorium, and I wait around a little bit so I can sit with Maverick and Fordo. I'm wearing a backward black ball cap with a heart and the word "Mother's" on it. My cousin Beezer gave it to me. I don't know how he has access to such hats. I don't ask. It is, without a doubt, the coolest thing in my personal wardrobe.

I sign Dr. Warren's clipboard and strongly consider leaving, but then the lights go down and I see *her*. The room is pitch black except for a spotlight on a girl onstage wearing a red velvet dress.

What? I thought this was going to be a bunch of boring kids reading boring poems in "poet voice." Poet voice is a whispery, super-serious voice that takes itself super seriously.

The girl is beautiful but in a completely different way. I'm mesmerized. She's not conventionally hot. Rather, she's...*interesting*. She has big eyes and full lips. She's maybe even a little weird looking—in the best possible way.

She looks like she enjoys life. I sink an elbow into Fordo's ribs.

I try Maverick and even Coppock. Nobody knows. I text Beezer, who's in high school, and who's sitting in another section.

I wait for what seems like forever. She's still belting out the poetry.

I get halfway through another text. "Dude, maybe you didn't ge—"

I don't respond.

Why? I'm not sure why. I can't even talk to a girl in my own grade. What am I going to do with a ninth grader? But she's homeschooled, which helps with the intimidation factor. I feel like a homeschooled ninth grader is like a regular eighth grader. That still puts her out of my league.

All of the guys are texting each other and giggling and getting dirty looks from Dr. Warren. I just stare intently at the stage. I'm staring at KK, for sure, but also at the fact that not all poetry is dumb and boring. I'm totally going to the library to check out this guy's complete collection after this is over.

In my school, it's really important to have a girlfriend. Having a girlfriend means you always have somebody to have lunch with and go to dances with.

I guess more deeply it's kind of validating to feel like somebody likes you in that way. I've never had a girlfriend. But in my defense, I've never really tried.

To be honest, I dream about having a girlfriend. I dream about having somebody in the stands wearing my jersey on game nights.

But I wonder if maybe I want a girlfriend just so that somebody will always be there to worship me or at least tell me, "Good job." This strikes me as a really bad reason to ask someone out.

Mimi always tries to explain, on the rare occasions that we talk about it. "Especially if she's the wrong girl, and especially if she doesn't love the Lord."

I know Mimi is right...but still.

The reading is over, but I wish there was more. There is a reception afterward in the cafeteria, and KK is serving food. I take a deep breath and decide to go through her line. I'm not hungry—I just want to be a little bit closer to her.

My face flushes as I get near her. She smiles and puts some food on my plate.

Oh my goodness.

Stunned silence. I'm shocked that I even register on her radar. She looks at me, expecting something in return.

I have nothing.

THE CARL SANDBURG
POETRY BOOK...

...weighs, like, 20 pounds. Just saying. It makes my backpack sag down and hurts my shoulder a little. But I feel smarter just by having it.

The librarian gives me an impressed look when I check it out. I'm killing it.

DREAMS GO ON: EMPTY FACTORY VERSUS MARION

A lot of people think a football player's pregame ritual involves, like, drinking animal blood or pounding your head against a locker.

Mine is the same every time. My mom, Mimi, puts some hymns on the stereo and tapes up my feet. I have blisters. Really bad blisters. I've gotten them every football season, regardless of what kind of cleats I wear. The hymns are supposed to calm me down.

That's the problem. When you're a football player, you don't want sensitive anything. She gently puts some lube on my heels, then a layer of Band-Aids, and then a layer of athletic tape. It's as close as she'll ever get to engaging me in football. But it's a really important step.

The first time I went to a pro football game with Pops—at the Hoosier Dome in Indianapolis—I was so excited that I hyperventilated during warm-ups. I had to breathe into a bag and almost threw up.

I said to Pops, "I'm going to do that someday." His response was perfect—he just smiled. He didn't kill my dream. But he also didn't promise I'd make it.

I love warm-ups. I love the piped-in music. I love that my uniform is clean and perfect.

Marion Middle School is a bigger school in a bigger town about 30 minutes away. They have bigger players. They step off their bus in uniforms that look just like the University of Michigan's, head to toe. They have the winged helmets and matching Nikes.

Our uniforms look like old, dirty hand-me-downs from the high school...because they are old, dirty hand-me-downs from the high school.

Did I mention that their players are gigantic? They're gigantic in both size and numbers. They probably have 50 players whereas we have 20.

I'm on the kickoff, kickoff return, punt, and punt return teams, in addition to playing offense and defense. Which is basically another way of saying I'm gonna die this afternoon.

After warm-ups we head back into our locker room. I make a beeline for the bathroom to be sick. This is a pregame ritual.

I'm so nervous, it's like my body is rejecting the idea of me being here and doing this at all.

I sit on a bench in the locker room just staring really intently at our red helmets. There's a white Bruin paw sticker on the side. My helmet is really scratched up. A point of pride.

What am I afraid of exactly? I don't know. Messing up in front of everybody? Collapsing because I'm so tired? I know I'm not afraid of any of the Marion Giants (that's their nickname—really). I guess I'm just afraid to fail. I'm afraid that I won't be good at this and that I'll never be good at anything.

I close my eyes and ask God to calm me down. (He doesn't.)

My plan for all of this is that God will make me a great football player so I can use the fame to share the gospel. By that I mean kneeling in the end zone after all my touchdowns and drawing a cross on my wrist tape. He knows that, though. I'm just waiting for it (being great) to kick in.

I remind myself that in three hours this will all be over.

And this is a thing that I love?

Coach Wood's red face is even redder than normal. "FLEX! Lead us in the prayer."

I kneel on the cold concrete and grab a teammate's hand.

And this is how Jesus taught people how to pray. Everything in there is the opposite of what we're about to go and do. If I was really forgiving those who trespassed against me, I'm not sure I'd be doing this.

"…for Thine is the kingdom, the power, and the glory forever. Amen."

Everybody screams at the end. That's how it always goes. We scream and swear and charge out the red door.

Ten minutes later, we're down 14-0.

I'm not even sure how it happens.

Marion has a running back that looks like he's going to declare for the NFL draft after the season. They have a lineman who has a beard and a tattoo!

We're seventh graders! Somebody check that kid's birth certificate!

To say we're a little intimidated would be an understatement. A guy comes back to the huddle at one point whimpering. Not full-on crying...but just like a quiet whimper. That's almost worse.

More whimpers.

At halftime we're down 28-0, and on my way off the field I sneak a look at the bleachers. Pops is sitting by himself as usual, far away from the Dead Coaches Society along the fence. He looks miserable. Mimi is crocheting a blanket. This is her nervous habit.

I look for KK, the mysterious reader's theater girl. Why would she be here? Why would she ever go to a seventh-grade football game? Tiffany is standing with a pack of girls with her back to the field.

Here's a brief synopsis of halftime: Coach Wood throws a Gatorade jug in frustration and says a bunch of words I can't repeat here.

The second half is much like the first except for one thing. In the third quarter the Marion quarterback drops back to pass. I come off the edge on a blitz and hit him—hard—right after he releases the ball. I get him right under the chin strap. When we hit the ground I can feel the air leave his lungs. He stays down for a second, but I pop right up and give out an impromptu scream.

Maverick pounds me on the helmet. I instinctively look up to the stands, where Pops gives me a thumbs-up.

The first thing you feel after a football game is relief that it's over and you survived.

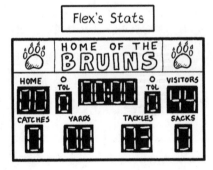

I take inventory of my bruises in the locker room. Because I play right outside linebacker, my left arm is bruised from shoulder to wrist—it's the arm I use to take on all the blockers. I've got a scrape on my left knee. My neck hurts, which is normal. Otherwise I'm none the worse for wear.

He says this after every game, whether I play well or not. He's scowling. Pops takes losing hard. Real hard. Mimi gives him his space. Pops has this expression on his face that says, "There's a lot I'm not saying."

I'm always looking for a little bit more from him though. Pops doesn't exactly throw compliments around easily.

I stay silent.

What about me? I decide to go the pathetic route and fish for a compliment.

A smile spreads across his face.

Indeed I did.

BASEMENT LAND:
BEEZER TALKS

The thing about Beezer's basement is the wrestling magazines. They're everywhere. Cheap newsprint paper. Black-and-white photos. Garish covers featuring guys like "Adorable" Adrian Adonis, "The Nature Boy" Ric Flair, Brutus "The Barber" Beefcake, and "Ravishing" Ric Rude. They're ridiculous but oddly compelling.

His basement is a shrine to what he loves—guitars, heavy metal (Metallica, Pantera), football (Dallas Cowboys, Chicago Bears jerseys), and wrestling.

Beezer's family went through a tough time a couple of years ago, and this basement sort of became his sanctuary. He retreated here to heal up. It kind of became a hospital. People left him alone down here to get better, and when he finally came out, he was a grown man—a guitar player.

He explains this in a completely unself-conscious way. He's not embarrassed about it. This is what's great about how we talk. We used to build wrestling rings in the backyard and film ourselves doing wrestling moves and having imaginary matches. And by "used to" I mean we did it last month.

I get it about the superhero thing. I think that's why I play sports. On the off chance that maybe, if you're good enough, somebody will remember you.

He picks out a Metallica riff on the guitar.

Nostalgic things about Beezer: The floors are littered with stacks of CDs because he listens to CDs and not MP3s. On one doorknob hangs one of those six-pack things and a single can of Mountain Dew—it was the last thing our Gramps bought him before Gramps died.

A babyface is a good guy. A heel is a bad guy.

Which isn't entirely untrue.

"Do you think people are basically good or basically bad?" I ask.

Again, this is the kind of thing you can ask in the basement. We turn into semi-philosophers down here. The reason I ask is that our church teaches that man is "totally depraved" apart from

God—meaning that in ourselves we aren't capable of anything pure. I'm not sure what I think about it. But I think I agree.

"Do you think people are born bad?" I ask again. I really need to figure this out.

One of the last things we did with Gramps was watch WrestleMania. He bought it for us on pay-per-view.

My two favorite wrestlers fought each other in the main event. I was so nervous I couldn't watch. I went back into Gramps's bedroom and read a book while Beezer shouted updates to me down the hall. The Gramps thing makes sense, but the Bible says that no man is righteous—not even one.

I'm not totally sure either. I guess it makes sense that apart from God, all people are bad. I mean, I technically know God, but I'm still bad a lot of the time.

Meaning?

Meaning my motives. The reasons I do things.

The way that even when I'm being good, I want people to, like, NOTICE me being good. The fact that when I want something, I have a tendency to do anything to get it.

I know what you mean.

What about Mimi and Pops? They're Christians. What would they say?

I decide not to focus on Mimi and Pops. They would say that once you know Jesus, you are "good" forever, in terms of not going to hell. Which is a good thing. Nobody wants to go to hell. The thing is, I know that Jesus exists and believe that He's real—in which case, I guess, I'm not going to hell. But what I struggle with is actually worshipping. I don't know how to feel like I actually know or love Jesus.

And that's why Beezer would be a heel.

"Dude," I ask. "What do you think of KK?"

YOUTH GROUP: SMELLS LIKE TEEN AWKWARDNESS

H ere's youth group in five words:

1. Basketball (our church has a gym).

2. Snacks (self-evident).

3. Rules (our youth director telling us what not to do in order to be a good Christian).

Appearance of our youth director: too much hair product, Jesus fish tattoo on ankle, too old to be wearing a necklace but wearing one anyway.

4. Watson (Watson is guitar-boy).

The girls love Watson, who takes his shirt off all the time and plays an acoustic guitar and manages to be both athletic and sensitive. As a result of this, all of the guys hate Watson. He looks like the kind of guy who plays high school tennis, because he *is* the kind of guy who plays high school tennis.

5. Waiting (for the prayer time to get over).

We sit on the all-purpose basketball-floor carpet, in a circle, as the talkative kids in the youth group say their prayer requests out loud and talk about them in great detail. Then we all bow our heads and close our eyes as the talkative kids say all the same things again except with their heads bowed and their eyes closed.

I feel SO TRAPPED by this whole thing. I have a hard time keeping my eyes closed in a group of my peers. I feel a very strong urge to stand up and just run out of the room. (I might actually do this. It's 50/50 in terms of me doing this at some point.)

TRANSCRIPT OF A TEXT EXCHANGE WITH WATSON FROM YOUTH GROUP, WHO INEXPLICABLY TEXTS ME SOMETIMES

Note: He's homeschooled.

I don't respond for a couple minutes because I don't know what to say.

Note: By "crazy" he means awesome.

She's okay.

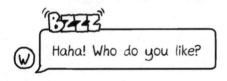

Haha! Who do you like?

This is a tough one. Guys like Watson are always asking questions like this. Then they'll take the information and either (a) use it against me somehow or (b) just use it to make fun of me during this conversation. What I mean is that there's really no good way to answer this question. I decide to throw it back to Watson by mentioning the name of a girl he for sure won't know.

The phone is silent for a couple minutes, during which I chew all of my fingernails completely to the nub. Not really, but that's how I'm feeling.

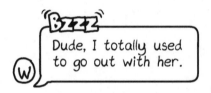

(That sound you hear is the sound of my heart breaking and also the sound of me losing all hope and my entire will to live.)

THINGS FALL APART

It's hard to focus on anything after the bomb that Watson dropped via text. But Pops and I do our usual evening routine, which consists of me running pass patterns and Pops throwing me passes. Tonight there is a little extra rage in my running, and I'm faster than usual.

I can see the look of surprise on Pops's face.

The thing is, I want to work so hard that I literally collapse and am unable to think or feel. That's how I'm dealing with the text from Watson. I just can't deal with a world in which somebody like her (beautiful and interesting) would date a preening schoolboy punk like Watson. It makes me sick to my stomach.

I run one last, hard fly pattern. A fly is where you just take off as hard as you can down the field and the quarterback just lofts it up there.

I gather it in without breaking stride and then lay down in the end zone (and by "end zone" I mean the edge of Johnny Hoeft's yard).

"You're a good tight end, Flex," Pops says on our way back in.

TOTAL ECLIPSE OF THE HEART

I'm dressing under the asbestos pipes. Just the end of another Wednesday practice. I hang my helmet on the kind of depressing wall hook that Rocky got his gear hung on when Mick gave his locker to another guy in *Rocky*. Coach Wood comes sidling up, full of Intensity and Pride.

I don't look up from my shoes, which have suddenly become very interesting. Meeting Coach Wood's gaze is sort of like looking right into the sun during a solar eclipse (the one that burns your eyes out).

"Which is why I'm moving you to center for the game against Madison-Grant," he says. "We've got McDermott hurt, and we need a guy who can snap and block. We can run behind you. You're the guy." He claps a big, meaty hand on my shoulder so hard that it hurts.

The fact of the matter is that I'm heartbroken. I don't want to play center. I haven't been running routes with Pops all summer so I can play center.

Centers can't catch passes. Centers don't score touchdowns. Centers wear numbers like 62—the worst number in all of football because nobody's body looks good in 62. Centers don't have girl-friends who wear their jerseys in the stands.

KK/Tiffany won't notice me if I'm wearing 62 and snapping a ball.

This is a nightmare. (Not compared to, like, nuclear war or famine or poverty, but you get my drift.)

I say this because I am a people pleaser, and for some reason I care about Coach Wood's feelings more than my own, even in this situation.

He tosses me a red mesh jersey with the number 62 on it. Of course.

The ride home is a blur. Not even proximity to George Blake's sister can make it better.

I mumble a hello to Mimi and Pops and then shut the door to my room, where I put on a depressing record (the Cure—mope rock) and mope.

I pull out a pro football magazine and look at the size of the centers.

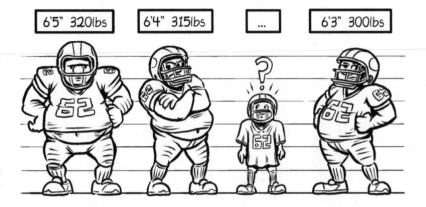

I'll never be that big. I'll never make the league as a center.

I throw the magazine across the room, and the, like, binding makes a little chunk in the drywall, for which I immediately feel guilty. I think about spackling it over but don't.

If you're scoring at home, here's what I've learned the past two days: That the new object of my fascination (KK) once dated the guy who I imagine beating up (Watson) when I'm listening to heavy metal music. And that I've changed positions.

Pops sticks his head in the door to tell me it's dinnertime.

He can tell something is up.

"Nothing." I stick with "nothing" for about five seconds.

Pops flops on my bed. "It's okay, man," he says after a while. "It's okay because you're still in the arena. You're still on the field. You're touching the ball on every play. You're making an impact. This is a learning experience, and it's a chance to serve your team. They need you. A lot of kids in that school would kill for a chance to just be on the field."

He's right, of course. But it doesn't work at all.

GOOD GAME(?): EMPTY FACTORY VERSUS MADISON-GRANT

I t's cold at Madison-Grant. Like so cold that the parents are shivering under the blankets and no kids made the trip to see the game.

No Tiffany. Of course, no KK. She remains a mystery. I don't even know where to go to run into her.

It's cancer awareness month, so we're wearing pink socks that look ridiculous because they clash with our red jerseys.

My new jersey, 62, is two sizes too big. Maverick catches me taping the sleeves shut in the locker room. This is done by grabbing a wad of fabric and winding a piece of athletic tape around it.

If you do anything out of the ordinary on a football team, you are automatically trying to be the Show. And you get made fun of for it. Sometimes I hate this sport.

I play the worst game of my life because I spend most of it just standing around chewing on my mouthpiece. I don't even get into a good stance on defense, and I let people run by me.

Pops isn't a yeller, but several times I hear him shout,

He paces up and down the sidelines outside the fence until sometime in the third quarter, when he gives up and starts playing catch with some random kid with a Nerf ball. He's playing catch with the Nerf kid because he's disgusted with my performance.

On the field the Madison-Grant guys are straight-up laughing at us. They're taunting us. I can see their smiles behind their face masks. Their coach is laughing on the sideline.

In fact, he let his starters go into the locker room halfway through the game and change into their street clothes. They're standing on the sidelines in their jeans and laughing at us.

What's weird is that they're just like we are. They watch the same shows at night. They eat the same junk food. Their girls look like our girls. They all detassel corn in the summers like us. My reaction to them laughing should be to bust their faces open. I should want that. But today I just don't have the heart to do it.

We lose 28-7. Here's my stat line:

```
┌─────────────────────────────────────┐
│   INDIVIDUAL PLAYER STATS            │
│  ┌──────────────────────┬────────┐   │
│  │ NAME                 │   #    │   │
│  │ FLEX                 │   62   │   │
│  ├──────────────────────┼────────┤   │
│  │            CATCHES   │   0    │   │
│  │            TACKLES   │   0    │   │
│  │             SACKS    │   0    │   │
│  │  FORCED FUMBLES      │   0    │   │
│  │  INTERNAL TANTRUMS   │ ▓▓▓▓   │   │
│  └──────────────────────┴────────┘   │
│      TOO MANY TO COUNT! ♪            │
└─────────────────────────────────────┘
```

Usually after every game, Pops will come up and put his arm around me and say, "Good game." Usually, after every game, I'm spent and tired, and regardless of whether I made any big plays, I feel really good about Pops doing this.

Today he just walks silently to the car with a look on his face that isn't a scowl but definitely isn't a smile either. Mimi is tense because Pops is tense. I'm tense because they're both tense.

Pops just throws the car into drive (angrily) and takes off. The ice-cream comment goes nowhere.

Because our house is small, I can hear them talking later that evening. I hear snatches of the conversation.

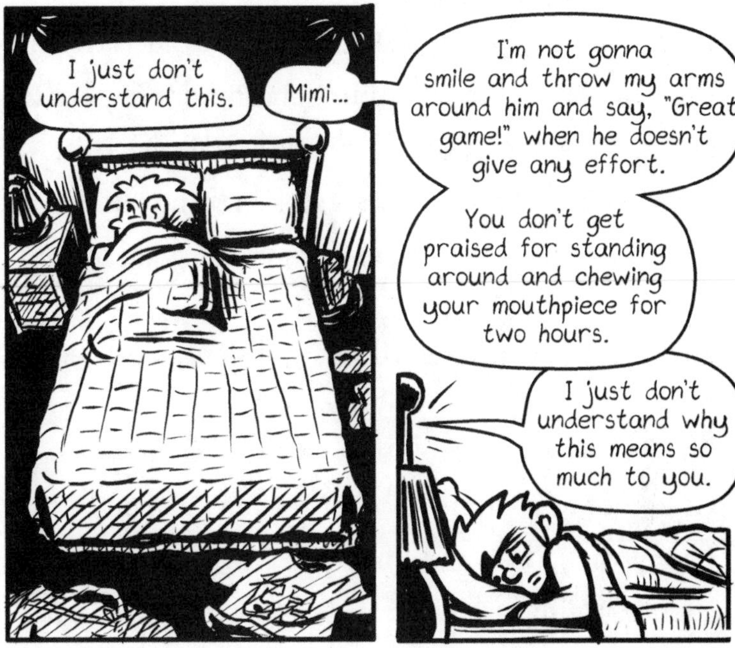
I just don't understand this.
Mimi...
I'm not gonna smile and throw my arms around him and say, "Great game!" when he doesn't give any effort.
You don't get praised for standing around and chewing your mouthpiece for two hours.
I just don't understand why this means so much to you.

Awkward silence.

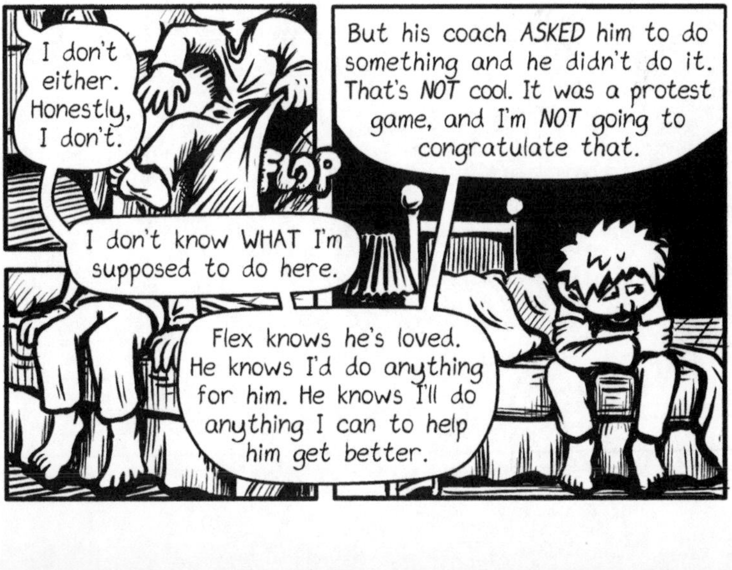
I don't either. Honestly, I don't.
FLOP
But his coach ASKED him to do something and he didn't do it. That's NOT cool. It was a protest game, and I'm NOT going to congratulate that.
I don't know WHAT I'm supposed to do here.
Flex knows he's loved. He knows I'd do anything for him. He knows I'll do anything I can to help him get better.

What's hardest about that is that I know he's right. And that even though I didn't play hard today I'm still sick about the loss. Losing is hard because it feels like something has been taken from you. An experience has been taken from you. A good feeling.

People say things like, "It's okay, it's only a game."

But the thing is, it's not only a game. Madison-Grant got to go home tonight feeling good and happy and jaunty and confident. We drove home in silence, feeling ashamed and like we'd failed. It's not just a game at that point. It's a period of time in our lives we'll never get back.

They won and we lost. And I hate it.

PIZZA KING

After the games we all go to a place called Pizza King.

Here's all you need to know about Pizza King: The decor hasn't changed in 30 years (according to Pops), and each booth has a phone you use to call your order directly to the kitchen. As you can imagine, this is fun. Also fun is the old Mortal Kombat game at the front. Also fun is the jukebox, which stopped updating its library around 1993.

The guys with girlfriends (like, three guys) bring their girlfriends, and the rest of us just eat pizza and talk about the game. Needless to say, I'm not in a talkative mood tonight.

The not-typical thing about Pizza King tonight is that KK is here. She's in a booth with a guy I've never seen before. He's wearing skinny jeans, ironic Chuck Taylors, and a hat that was knitted out of yarn.

These factors, combined with my current mood, make him the kind of guy I want to punch.

I don't know how I should feel in these moments. I know, because of church, that I should theoretically be happy because of Christ and because I'm going to heaven. But right now I don't feel joyful. I know that I shouldn't worry about my future, because God is in all of it. But still. I envision a life where I don't play college football and, therefore, don't even want to go to college.

Not even my dad thinks I can play anymore. I envision lots of meals alone.

My friends leave. It'll be a few more minutes before my folks come to get me, so I just sit in the booth alone.

I imagine what it will be like to sit in this booth when I'm 30 and single. No wife, no kids, no glory days to reflect on.

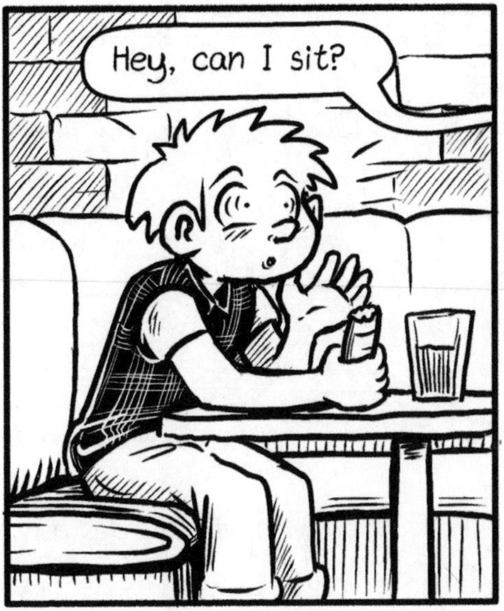
Hey, can I sit?

She's already, in fact, seated when she asks this. It's KK.

She's wearing a baggy '90s sweater and totally pulling it off. I'm wearing a pair of jeans, work boots, and a flannel shirt that I cut the sleeves out of. I feel underdressed and ridiculous.

He looks like the guy who will one day buy a motor-cycle for all the wrong reasons. His heart won't really be in it.

I almost knock a glass of Sprite over due to how emphatic I am about her not leaving. She readjusts in the booth and does this superhot thing girls do, which is to sit sideways in the booth and pull their knees up to their chest.

"Let me ask you a question," she says. "If you were married to someone, and you died, would you want your girl to remarry?"

What kind of a question is this? What I like about it, however, is that it's not about football.

She smiles. This seems to please her. Then she takes a drag on my Sprite.

"What kind of music do you like?" she asks.

I name a few bands that I've heard in Beezer's basement, figuring that if they're cool enough for him, they might be cool enough for her. She smiles again.

By that I mean I'll probably spend about six hours on it, starting the moment I arrive home tonight. And by "playlist" I mean I'll actually burn it onto a CD so that she has something that came from my house.

POPS CAN'T SLEEP

I hear him rattling around in the kitchen at, like, two a.m. I stumble out and sit at the table.

I know he's having trouble sleeping not just because of the loss but because of the kind of loss it was. It killed Pops that the Madison-Grant kids were

dancing around and laughing and waving their fingers at our bench and our fans. In the economy of Pops, this is unacceptable. In the economy of Pops, you die before you let this happen. How do I know this? Because he said,

That's a direct quote.

Pops is wired a little differently from most people.
He was so mad after the game that he couldn't look
at me or even touch me. He couldn't give me a hug.
Couldn't put his arm around me. I know it killed him
to see me walking through the handshake line afterward and shaking their hands. In the economy of
Pops, you don't shake the hand of someone who
has disrespected you like that. Pops got into a lot of
fights when he was younger, for this reason.

There are some losses where a better opponent just
beat you. And then there are losses like this, where
it seems like they took a part of your soul. Like they
dominated you in a way that's gross and unnatural.

When we were alone after the game, Pops said some things I knew he'd regret later. How did I know? Because I know Pops loves the Lord, and I know the man he's striving to be, if that makes sense. However, he doesn't always pull off being that man.

But he always apologizes.

The tea is called Sleepytime. It's weird to see some-body so big and aggressive drinking something called Sleepytime, whose logo is a really meek-looking bear in a nightshirt.

Pops is wearing a shirt from when he was in high school. It's an "Empty Factory High—Dome Day 1994" shirt. It has a bad silk-screened picture of the Hoosier Dome on it. It's threadbare, but he can't throw it away. Pops is a deeply nostalgic dude.

What he said were some really choice things about Madison-Grant's players and coaches, which I can't repeat here.

He hugs me. And I have to tell you, it feels really good. I feel like we're connected again. Pops isn't just my dad or a football player or a football coach. Pops is my best friend.

I go upstairs and climb back into bed, convinced again that Christianity is real. Because in real life, apart from God, people don't apologize.

SONGS ON KK'S MIX CD

I made the playlist by raiding the CDs in Beezer's basement and in the armrest of Pop's car.

PLAYLIST FOR K.K.
FROM FLEX

"HEAVEN" BY WARRANT
"I REMEMBER YOU" BY SKID ROW
"SHUT UP AND DANCE" BY WALK THE MOON
"THIS LOVE" BY PANTERA
"ANNA BEGINS" BY COUNTING CROWS
"I DON'T WANNA MISS A THING" BY AEROSMITH
"WHEN I SEE YOU SMILE" BY BAD ENGLISH

And an unfortunate 35-second interlude of me pouring my heart out to KK...verbally, on the recording. I immediately regret this as soon as I give Beezer the CD to give to her.

VACATION DAY: FLEX CONFRONTS COACH WOOD

I hurt my knee in Tuesday's practice. A guy fell right on it in a pile and it hyperextended, which is just a fancy way of saying that it bent the wrong way.

The doctor said to take it easy for a couple of days, so today I'm in street clothes. In sports contexts, people always say "street clothes." It's another way to say "jeans and a T-shirt."

Coach Wood is in his usual place behind the offense, exuding Pride and Intensity. He keeps up a steady stream of banter during practice. He spits on the ground all the time, which is weird because he's not eating sunflower seeds or chewing tobacco. It's like a reflex. He turns in my direction.

Everybody guffaws. Har har. Middle school pack-mentality laughter.

My face immediately turns red hot. I'm beyond embarrassed and mad because if anybody loves football it's me. I've never missed a weight-lifting or running session. I have no response for Coach Wood, and when I work up the courage to look at him, he's twirling his whistle around his finger. He probably forgot the whole thing about ten seconds after it left his mouth.

Not me.

I slump on the sofa after practice, fighting back tears.

And then I explain the whole thing to Mimi and Pops. Mimi gives me a huge hug because she's Mimi. It's embarrassing, but I cry into her shoulder.

Pops is silent for a minute. I know he'd go to war for me, no matter what. Ride or die. That's Pops.

"I think you should call him," Pops says. "It's part of being a man and part of being on a team. I can't fight your battles for you. I can't go to your coach. It wouldn't be appropriate. Matthew 18 says that if you feel like somebody has wronged you, you should go to them and address it."

I'm terrified. Pops tosses his phone onto the sofa. I also know he's right. If he fought my battles for me, he'd be no different from the dads in the Dead Coaches Society.

"I'll pray with you if you want," he says. "It'll be okay."

He prays. I dial. My fingers tremble as I push the numbers. I really hope it rings through and I get a machine.

I wonder what such a prideful, intense man does in his spare time. From the sound of the background noise, my guess would be watching TV and heating something up in the microwave. Not exactly what I expected.

I'm nervous-talking, which means I'm continuing to talk for fear of awkward silence.

And that is that. I'm not sure if it's the kind of phone call Coach will laugh about with all the other coaches. Like a "Listen to what this idiot called me about!" kind of thing. I guess it doesn't matter to me either way. I'm still glad I called.

LADYBUG SUNDRESS: THE KK STORY

I delivered the CD to KK via Beezer. It's really scary to put yourself out there like that. I wrapped it in notebook paper after painstakingly writing the song titles on a tiny sticker. I heard from her a few days later via a returned note:

I loved the CD!
Dinner this Saturday?
I'll pick you up at six.
<u>I'm cooking!</u> ☺

K.K.

Who cooks? Who does this on a date? And how can somebody who doesn't drive yet pick me up? So many questions.

I am ready in my nicest jeans and button-down shirt at five forty-five, seated ramrod straight on the sofa and checking the time roughly every five seconds.

There is aftershave involved. I probably smell like I bathed in it.

Six p.m. comes and goes. As does six fifteen. KK and I have a "vintage" relationship, which is just a fancy way to say we don't text. The thing is, I don't even have her number. And I'm not sure how Mimi and Pops would feel about me texting a girl.

I envision her wrapped in Watson's shirtless arms. He's probably someplace serenading her with his acoustic guitar right now. They're probably going to get married.

I hate life. I hate everything. How could I be so stupid? How could I allow myself to hope?

She does the thing that some people do where she rings the doorbell and then opens the door up a little before anything happens. Incredibly brazen.

She smells like someplace exotic. She's backlit by a rare sunny evening and is wearing a sundress with ladybugs printed on it. There's a car idling in the driveway, driven by a guy.

"My brother," she says, reading my mind.

He looks like a banker and is reading the financial section of the *Muncie Star*.

Not a threat.

He drives us to her house, where the amazing smells of dinner waft from the kitchen. She asks me to pick some music for dinner, and I pick the only artist I've actually heard of. Tracy Chapman. Crisis averted. She then makes dazzling conversation for a really long time, and by that I mean she asks me a lot of great questions. I try to ask her great questions back.

Finally, I ask,

To which she looks me straight in the eye and replies,

She smiles. It is, of course, the perfect answer.

Part of the date is for her to visit a Catholic church service for a comparative religions class she's taking. She gets the times wrong, and it's empty. She seems to really struggle with time.

We sit in the church and talk for hours. Catholic churches are beautiful in a way that mine isn't. By that I mean mine looks like a concrete bunker and they look...well...beautiful. Lots of stained-glass windows and Gothic stuff.

It makes you feel like you're really in a church. It's dark in here, sort of. There are lots of nice shadows, and streetlights stream in through the stained glass. It looks cool.

"Let me rifle through your wallet," she says. It was only a year ago that I transitioned out of an Indianapolis Colts wallet with Velcro. Close call.

At some point I grab her hand.

It feels amazing. Her hand in mine. This is a first.

"Let's go for a walk," she says.

We're still holding hands. She walks me to a gas station, where she buys me a bottle of really cheap-looking pop.

She laughs.

"It was really popular in Michigan, where I used to live," she explains.

It tastes delicious, primarily because it's from her.

After her brother drops me off later that night, our neighborhood is dark and quiet. I don't want the night to end, so I just take a walk. I walk around my block several times, right down the middle of the street.

I feel like the king of the world. A gunfighter. A warrior. I feel like I can do anything.

I walk by Mitch Warner's backyard, where we used to spray-paint lines on the grass and play football in gear that was too big for us. We pretended to be our favorite guys (LeGarrette Blount for me).

I walk by Timmy Walter's driveway, where we play hours of pickup basketball, even in the winter with frozen hands, with each of us pretending to be our favorite guy (Boris Diaw for me because he reads books).

I walk by Chuck Hidy's house, where he and his dad are always working on a car.

I love it here.

RIDE OR DIE: EMPTY FACTORY AT MADISON-GRANT (PLAYOFFS)

In middle school football, everybody makes the playoffs. It is, as they say, a new season. My knee is feeling better, and I've even made my peace with playing center. It is what it is. I tape my sleeves in the locker room and nobody gives me any grief about trying to be the Show.

Everybody is too nervous. We're all in our own heads.

Pops prayed with me before the game. It was as much a prayer for himself as for me.

Mimi seemed pleased by this development.

A guy named Whitey—one of our starting linebackers—has a boom box in the locker room. It plays a song called "Symphony of Destruction" on repeat. Here's all you need to know about Whitey: He's in eighth grade and has a moustache.

I walk to the bathroom to puke. I am now ready.

Warm-ups. My dad is alone by the fence. He gives me a little thumbs-up and smiles.

I think I probably will. Pops can't help himself. Football makes him aggressive.

Tiffany is standing with a pack of girls, all of whom are giggling with their backs to the field. It probably smells like hair product over there. KK—my KK—is on the top row of the bleachers with a book next to her, surrounded by yarn and crochet needles.

She is one of a kind.

The game is physical. I am on the kickoff return team, as a blocker, and I catch a guy who's screaming down the field, not looking at me. I catch

him in his earhole and he goes flying. The crowd goes "Ooh!" I can hear the air leave his body as he hits the ground.

It's almost halftime and the score is still 0-0.

I'm playing outside linebacker, and a guy named Allen on the other team has been blocking me dirty all night. Here's all you need to know about Allen: He wears a visor on his helmet.

He's trying to be the Show.

Football is a rough game.

I sit on the cold concrete floor of the locker room while a trainer shoves cotton up my nose.

I catch Whitey's eye, and he nods approvingly. I think I'm a man now. I think this is what it feels like.

I don't think I've ever been happier as a football player.

Coach Wood squats down next to me with a whiteboard. He seems happy with my Intensity and Pride.

Flex, we got a little change of plans for the second half.

We're gonna simplify.

I'm putting Maverick at quarterback, and he's gonna run a quarterback sneak behind you on every play.

When he comes to the line of scrimmage he's just gonna tap you on the hip, and you'll block their nose guard the opposite way.

TAP

It's our only shot at moving the ball.

"Got it, Coach," I reply.

Their nose guard is a big blond-haired kid named Amick who looks like he's thrown a lot of hay bales in his day.

Amick

Our guys have a nickname for Amick that I can't print here because it wouldn't be fair to the kid or his family.

I settle into my stance over the ball, and lo and behold, Maverick taps me on the hip. I fire off into Amick, and I can feel Mav behind me, grinding out the yards.

Five yards on first down. Four yards on second down. Six yards on third down.

We run quarterback sneaks all the way down the field and into the end zone. We miss the extra point.

Every time we kick, Mav has to run to the sideline and put on this weird-looking square-toed shoe from the '70s. We call it the Club.

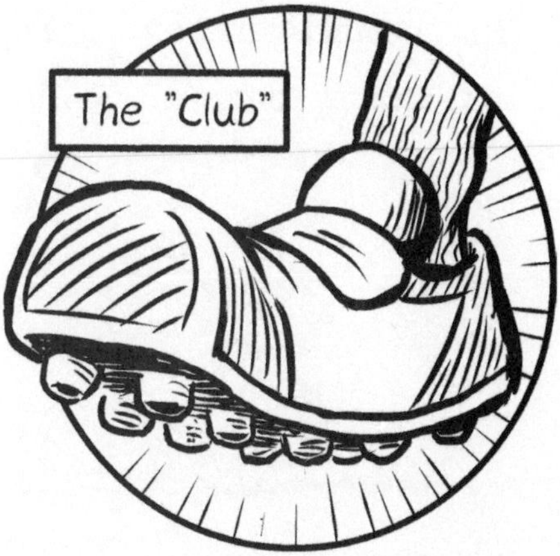
The "Club"

He kicks one off the side of his foot.

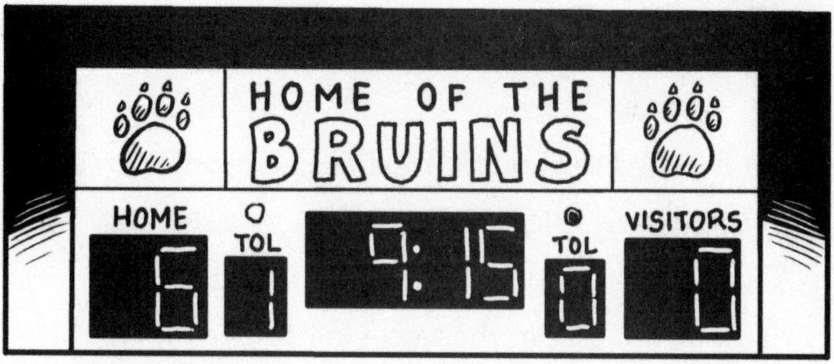
HOME OF THE
BRUINS
HOME
6
TOL
1
9:15
TOL
0
VISITORS
0

I'm suddenly really enjoying playing on the line!

As always, I'm playing offense and defense and all the special teams. It's unseasonably hot out here—probably 70 degrees and humid.

The thing I love about football is that when it's really working well—like now—you lose yourself in it. And the fans do too. I can tell by looking at Pops that nothing else in the world matters to him in this moment. This is the part of the game that people get addicted to.

Everything on me hurts. My legs are aching and sore. My head hurts. My mouth is dry, but the rest of my body is soaked with sweat.

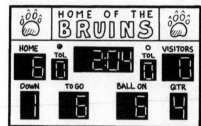

Madison-Grant has the ball and is driving. Our defense is tired.

Between plays we all bend over at the waist and just gulp air.

My favorite thing about football is that it's not sub-jective. That means that who wins a game isn't decided by judges. It's decided by the scoreboard. If we stop Madison-Grant here, we're better than them. It's just that simple. So many things in life—like popularity—are decided just by somebody's opinion. Football is real. It's so real. It might be the only real thing left.

If Madison-Grant scores here, they're better than us. If we stop them somehow, we're better than them. I may not know a whole lot about the world, but I'll at least know that much.

They have the ball, first and goal, from the six-yard line.

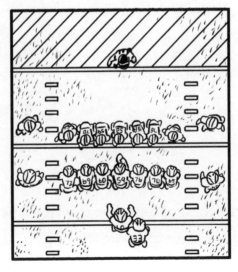

There are six yards between us going home winners or losers. Six yards between a good night and a bad night.

First down: Madison-Grant throws a fade to the back of the end zone. Incomplete. Those hardly ever work.

Madison-Grant has a stud running back named John Eden.

Last night I had a dream that Eden took a pitch and I slammed him in the backfield for a loss. Honestly, it's better than any play I've ever made in real life.

John Eden

Second down: They run a trap inside to Eden and one of our linemen trips him up. Gain of four. Third and goal on the two.

Third down: They try a bootleg pass to the opposite side of the field from me. Whitey jumps up and knocks it down at the line of scrimmage.

Fourth down: This is our whole season. It's quiet in the huddle and at the line of scrimmage.

Everybody is gasping for air and looking down. At the line of scrimmage I look into the eyes of the Madison-Grant guys. Everybody looks scared and tired. They look just like us. There are only two seconds left on the clock. I line up at my right outside linebacker position, on the outside shoulder of their tight end.

I look up at KK. She's standing now. No book. No crochet.

I look at Pops and he just nods.

Their quarterback screams out the cadence and reverse pivots. He tosses the ball to Eden coming to my side.

My job is to keep outside leverage on the tight end and turn the play back inside. I slam into the tight end with my left shoulder and easily throw him to the ground.

It's just me and Eden now. What's weird is that I can see his eyes and hear him breathing.

He's sprinting toward the pylon, and I'm sprinting toward him. I slam into him with my left shoulder and pick him up and slam him to the ground one yard short of the end zone.

The next few seconds are a blur.

I feel people smacking my helmet and dragging me to my feet. I shake Eden's hand and tell him good game. I actually kind of hug him, and he hugs me. I think we're both just glad to be done.

I'm suddenly filled with this feeling—I don't want him to have a bad night. He deserves to have a great night just like us.

"You're really good," is all I can think of in response. He smiles behind the helmet.

I rip off my helmet—it's so hot inside there—and just kind of flop down on my back in the end zone.

The grass is cool on my legs. It's a clear blue sky. My teammates are whooping and laughing on the field. I want to join them, but I also just want to lie here forever. My stomach is going up and down, drinking the air.

At the end of every practice we used to run 16 40-yard dashes. Everybody hated this. It felt like misery added to misery on a hot field that felt like concrete under our feet. I never came in first—not even close. But this is why we did it. So that we could be a little less tired at the end, when it mattered.

I'm glad Coach Wood made me do them, even though I thought he was sadistic and evil at the time. I'm glad I did them. He might still be sadistic and evil.

Pops is standing along the fence, looking at me lying there. Mimi has joined him, and he has his arm around her. KK smiles behind them.

I can tell Pops is looking at me, but I don't want him to know that I know. A moment later I feel his hand on my hair.

It's as proud as he's ever been of me.

I can tell.

ABOUT THE AUTHOR

Ted Kluck is an award-winning writer whose work has appeared in *ESPN the Magazine*, *Sports Spectrum Magazine*, and *ESPN.com*. He's the author of several books, including *Why We're Not Emergent: By Two Guys Who Should Be*, coauthored with Kevin DeYoung. Ted lives in Michigan with his wife, Kristin, and their two sons, Tristan and Maxim. www.tedkluck.com

ABOUT THE ARTIST

Daniel Hawkins is a freelance graphic designer and illustrator based in the Pacific Northwest. He earned his BFA in applied visual arts from Oregon State University. In addition to serving the worldwide mission of the Nike Foundation, he has worked as an independent contractor for a variety of local, national, and global organizations. www.dhawkdesign.com

To learn more about Harvest House books or
to read sample chapters, visit our website:

www.HarvestHousePublishers.com

HARVEST HOUSE PUBLISHERS
EUGENE, OREGON